Mr. Persnickety and Cat Lady

Story and pictures by

Paul Brett Johnson

ORCHARD BOOKS / NEW YORK

Orchard Books
A Grolier Company
95 Madison Avenue
New York, NY 10016

Manufactured in the United States of America
Printed and bound by Phoenix Color Corp.
Book design by Mina Greenstein
The text of this book is set in 14 point Cushing Book.
The illustrations are acrylic.

1 3 5 7 9 10 8 6 4 2

Library of Congress Cataloging-in-Publication Data
Johnson, Paul Brett.
Mr. Persnickety and Cat Lady / story and pictures by Paul Brett Johnson.
p. cm.
Summary: Mr. Persnickety objects to Cat Lady's many cats and resorts to
drastic action to get rid of them.
ISBN 0-531-30283-0 (tr. : alk. paper)—ISBN 0-531-33283-7 (lib. bdg. : alk. paper)
[1. Cats—Fiction. 2. Neighbors—Fiction.] I. Title.
PZ7.J6354 Mi 2000 [E]—dc21 99-56557

To good neighbors, cat lovers, and Joe

—P.B.J.

Mr. Persnickety and Cat Lady were next-door neighbors.

Mr. Persnickety always wore a bow tie (solid, of course). He kept a perfect lawn. And he had two well-behaved goldfish.

Cat Lady wore sneakers with holes in them. She grew dandelions.
And she had thirty-seven cats.

If asked, Cat Lady seemed to recall that Mr. Persnickety's real name was Alphonse or Egbert or something stuffy like that. Mr. Persnickety, on the other hand, was sure he did not remember Cat Lady's real name, nor did he care to.

The trouble had started back when Cat Lady took in her first cat. Mr. Persnickety disliked cats. They scared off his mourning doves, and they went to the bathroom in his tulip bed. Besides, Mr. Persnickety was allergic to cats. Or so he said.

"Excuse me, but that cat will have to go," called Mr. Persnickety.
"I don't like cats."

"I beg your pardon?" Cat Lady called back.

"I said, *I don't get along with cats!*"

Cat Lady could hardly believe Mr. Persnickety's nerve. "Well, I'm afraid that's too bad," she said. "Henrietta belonged to my dear Aunt Faye, may she rest in peace. Henrietta has no place else to go."

After Henrietta moved in, Cat Lady learned that she had a soft spot for cats. Fat cats, skinny cats, longhaired cats, shorthaired cats, hard-luck cats, purebreds. It didn't matter. Cat Lady loved them all.

Before she knew it, Cat Lady had a house full of them. They lounged on every available piece of furniture, including the TV. They required an extra grocery cart just for cat food and kitty litter. But Cat Lady didn't mind, because at night she had no need for a blanket, not even in winter.

Mr. Persnickety might have tolerated living next door to one cat. But two cats were out of the question. Five cats were unthinkable. Ten cats gave him fits. And thirty-seven meant war!

Mr. Persnickety sprayed Cat Lady's cats with the garden hose. While he was at it, he gave Cat Lady a good drenching as well.

"Ooops! Terribly sorry," said Mr. Persnickety. "Must have slipped."

Mr. Persnickety put on a tape recording of a hundred
barking dogs and turned it up full blast.

Cat Lady played her disco albums as loudly as they would go.

Mr. Persnickety called in a complaint to the Humane Society. "What a shame," he said. "All those poor, sweet kitty cats living cooped up together. There ought to be a law."

The Humane Society came to investigate. Afterward they gave Cat Lady an award for her excellent work with stray animals.

And so it went, on and on.

One day Mr. Persnickety mysteriously developed a mouse problem.

He bought a load of mousetraps. But these mice seemed to be especially clever. They stole the cheese from his traps without getting so much as a whisker caught.

Neither did poison do a bit of good. The mice multiplied like mushrooms. Soon there were mice in the clothes hamper. Mice in the bread box. Mice in the vacuum cleaner. Mice in the teacups.

When Mr. Persnickety found a nest inside his favorite teddy bear, he had finally had enough. But what could he do?

Mr. Persnickety forced himself to slink next door and ring the bell.

"Yes?" said Cat Lady as though she had not been expecting him.

"Uhhh. I was just wondering. Er. That is . . ."

"Cat got your tongue?" Cat Lady asked.

"Now, see here. I mean . . . these mice. . . . It's just that, if you wouldn't mind. . . ." No matter how hard he tried, Mr. Persnickety could not make the words come out.

"Would you like to borrow my cats?" Cat Lady finally asked.

Mr. Persnickety gave a sigh of relief. "Please."

"I'll think about it," said Cat Lady.

The next day
Cat Lady came
calling with all
thirty-seven cats.

There was an
eruption of mice.
In no time at all,
Mr. Persnickety's
house was free
of the appalling
critters.

"Thank you," Mr. Persnickety said in a small voice as Cat Lady
marched her cats back home. "By the way, my name is Albert."

Cat Lady stopped and turned around. She smiled. "How do you do, Albert. My name is Lucille."

From that day on, Mr. Persnickety and Cat Lady were perfect neighbors . . .

. . .well, for the most part.